THE JOHN J. WRIGHT LIBRARY
LA ROCHE COLLEGE
9000 Babcock Boulevard
Pittsburgh, PA   15237

Rosemary Wells

❧ PEABODY ❧

Dial Books for Young Readers

E. P. DUTTON, INC. *New York*

j W46 p

THE JOHN J. WRIGHT LIBRARY
LA ROCHE COLLEGE
9000 BABCOCK BLVD.
PITTSBURGH, PA 15237

Published by
Dial Books for Young Readers
A Division of E. P. Dutton, Inc.
2 Park Avenue
New York, New York 10016

Copyright © 1983 by Rosemary Wells
All rights reserved. Printed in the U.S.A.
Design by Atha Tehon

Library of Congress Cataloging in Publication Data
Wells, Rosemary.
Peabody.
Summary: Annie's affection for Peabody, her teddy bear,
is temporarily overshadowed by the novelty
of a new talking birthday doll.
[1. Teddy bears — Fiction. 2. Dolls — Fiction.] I. Title.
PZ7.W46843Pe 1983   [E]   83-7207
ISBN 0-8037-0004-0
ISBN 0-8037-0005-9 (lib. bdg.)

First Edition
(C O B E)
10 9 8 7 6 5 4 3 2 1

The art consists of watercolor paintings
that are camera-separated and
reproduced in full color.

For Miss P. Pod,
light of my life

Peabody had never been out of his big
yellow box until Annie's birthday.

"It's a real bear!" shouted Annie.

"Want it," said Annie's brother, Robert.

"Peabody bites," said Annie.

Annie gave a private party for Peabody,
because it was his birthday too.

Warmly dressed in one of Robert's old shirts, Peabody spent the night on Annie's pillow. "How lucky I am to be real," he said. "How happy I am to be Annie's."

Before she went to school, Annie always put Peabody
on her highest shelf. He made many new friends.
When Robert sneaked in and peeked, Peabody growled
at him. "Peabody bites," said Robert.

Annie taught Peabody how to ski on a pair of Popsicle
sticks. Snow got into his ears, but the exercise and
a woolen scarf kept him warm.

After a day on the slopes Peabody and Annie sipped hot chocolate with marshmallows and toasted their feet by the fire.

In April they started a garden with
pansies and dandelions.

The garden fence was made of bright red wool.
"That's an electric fence, Robert. Don't touch it!"
said Annie.

In July Peabody visited the shore with Annie and her family. Salty breezes from the sea tickled his nose.

Annie took him boating in the overturned shell of
a horseshoe crab. His sun umbrella came all the way
from China.

That autumn Peabody told all his friends on the shelf
about the seashore far away. He showed them the shells
he had collected there.

A thousand leaves fell to the ground in the winter wind.
Peabody's ears had lost some pinkness from skiing in
wet snow. He still had summer sand between his toes
and dried spring mud in his fur, but Annie said he
wasn't wearing out. He was wearing in.

On their birthday eve Peabody was too excited to
sleep. He watched the birthday moon rise and set over
the snow. Deep in the woods an owl hooted a song.

Peabody sang back while Annie slept. Blue-white
starlight filled Annie's room. In it Peabody danced
a birthday dance.

In the morning the first present Annie opened was
Rita. By turning a key somewhere on Rita's body Rita
could be made to talk and walk. She drank real apple
juice and sang three different songs.

When Robert wanted Rita, Annie made Rita howl like
a real baby.
That afternoon was perfect for skiing but they didn't
go because Rita was learning to walk across the
living room.

Rita completely ruined Peabody's birthday party.
She would not stop singing.

Sharing a bed with Rita was no picnic. During the
night Annie bumped Rita's key. "Good morning.
I love you! Good morning. I love you!" said Rita.

Snowy days came and went, but there was no skiing
and no hot chocolate and no fireplace to sit by. Even
Peabody's friends were quiet. He had shown them his
shells many times and there was nothing left to talk
about. One night Annie left Peabody on the shelf.

He woke up uncomfortable and grouchy. In a week a cobweb had grown along his arm and onto the wall. Inside Peabody there was a great sleepiness. Without Annie's love Peabody did not feel real. He did not feel alive. At night the owl hooted and sang from the woods but Peabody did not sing back.

Suddenly, after many weeks asleep on the shelf something woke Peabody up. "Good morning. I love you! Good morning. I love you!" said a voice. It was Rita. Robert had got hold of her.

He wound her up and gave her a cup of coffee.

After her coffee Robert gave Rita a bath.
The minute Rita hit the water she stopped talking.

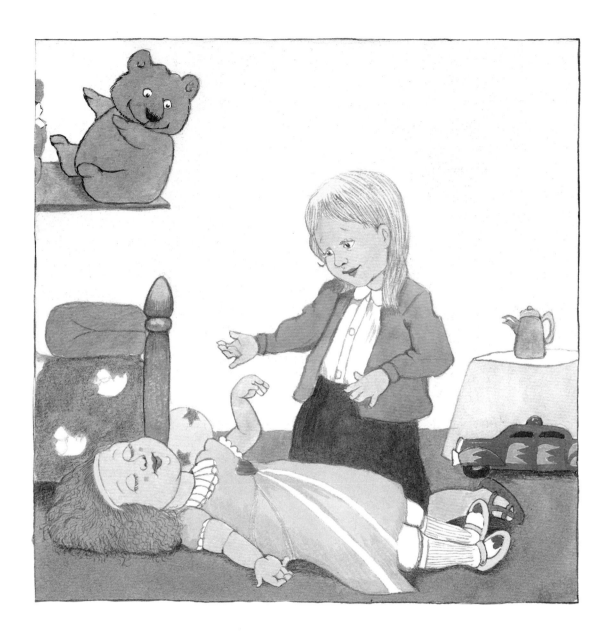

Rita looked clean and dry when Annie came home,
but inside her batteries and wires were wrecked.
Annie wound her up. Rita wouldn't do anything.

Peabody held out his arms to Annie.
"I need you," said Annie.

vnstdiJ nowell 2 nodel ncl

That night Rita stayed in Robert's crib.

The John J. Wright Library

And Peabody danced to the music of the spring rain.